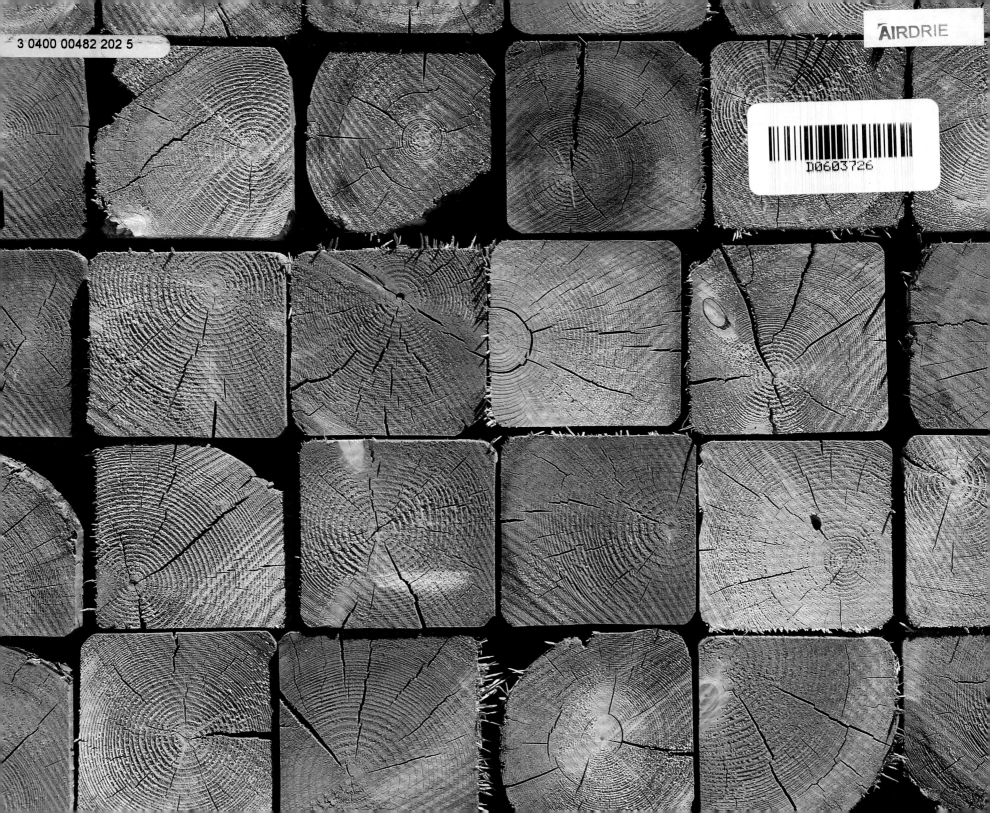

Forestry A-Z

by **Kathleen Cook Waldron** and **Ann Walsh**
photography by **Bob Warick**

ORCA BOOK PUBLISHERS

Library and Archives Canada Cataloguing in Publication

Walsh, Ann, 1942-
Forestry A-Z / written by Ann Walsh and Kathleen Cook
Waldron ; illustrated by Bob Warick.
ISBN 978-1-55143-504-6
1. Forests and forestry--Juvenile literature. I. Waldron, Kathleen Cook.
II. Warick, Bob, 1949- III. Title.
SD376.W35 2008   j634.9   C2007-906372-1

First published in the United States, 2008
Library of Congress Control Number: 2007939502

Summary: An introduction to modern forestry and its practices.

Orca Book Publishers gratefully acknowledges the support for its publishing programs provided by the following agencies: the
Government of Canada through the Book Publishing Industry Development Program and the Canada Council
for the Arts, and the Province of British Columbia through the BC Arts Council and the Book Publishing Tax Credit.

Cover and author photographs: Bob Warick
Design: Teresa Bubela

Interior photographs by Bob Warick except the following:
B – Breakup by Craig Hooper
F – Firefighting courtesy BC Fire Protection Branch, Ministry of Forests and Range
H – Helicopter logging courtesy Canadian Air-Crane Ltd.
I – Mountain pine beetle close-up courtesy Ministry of Forests and Range
J – Image I-58498 (top) courtesy of Royal BC Museum, BC Archives,
bottom image courtesy of City of Vancouver Archives, LP 255.4
Q – Images B-06976 (top) and D-00406 (bottom) courtesy of Royal BC Museum, BC Archives
O – Owl by Ed Robertson

ORCA BOOK PUBLISHERS   ORCA BOOK PUBLISHERS
PO Box 5626, STN. B   PO Box 468
VICTORIA, BC CANADA   CUSTER, WA USA
V8R 6S4   98240-0468

www.orcabook.com
Printed and bound in China.

11 10 09 08 • 4 3 2 1

This book is dedicated to the world's forests
and to all who work, play and live in them.
—Kathleen and Ann

To my mom and dad, for all their support.
—RSW

A

All kinds of trees, all kinds of forests, all around the world.

From aspens in the mountains to palm trees by the sea, from thousand-year-old cedars to freshly planted pines, forests grow on every continent except Antarctica. They are vital to life on earth. The influence of trees stretches far beyond the boundaries of the forest. The book you now hold in your hands was made possible through the science of modern forestry.

B

Bush work bogs down in breakup.

Work in the forest changes with the seasons. In northern countries, an in-between season called breakup begins when the snow melts and the ground thaws. In the bush—areas far from cities or highways—the earth becomes muddy and as soft as chocolate pudding. Unpaved roads can turn into slippery rivers of mud, and paved highways can buckle and heave like roller-coaster tracks. Heavy machinery and trucks will damage this ground, so logging stops. But soft spring earth is ideal for planting new trees.

ROAD

C

Carrying "cork" boots, the crew crowds around the crummy.

Tree-planting, logging, and other crews often ride to work in heavy-duty passenger trucks or vans called crummys. In the bush, the crummy may be the only shelter in a thunderstorm or blizzard, or the only black-fly- and mosquito-free lunchroom for miles.

Most crews wear rugged boots with steel toe-protectors and small sharp spikes in the soles. These cork boots or corks, usually spelled **c-a-u-l-k-s**, help workers climb over slippery logs and uneven ground.

D

Dawn to dusk is a logger's day.

Fallers cut trees along trails so logs can be moved—skidded—to a cleared area called a landing. Here workers called buckers remove the branches and tops and cut the logs into smaller pieces before they are loaded onto trucks.

Before chainsaws, loggers cut trees with handsaws and axes. Horses and oxen hauled them away. Now huge machines help with this dangerous work. Feller-bunchers fall the trees, skidders pull them to the landing, processors trim and stack them, and loaders put them on trucks.

E

Erosion eats away earth; trees ease erosion.

Erosion is the washing away of soil by water and wind. It occurs where there are no grasses, shrubs or trees to hold soil in place. All roots, whether as wide as a barrel or as thin as a hair, carry food and water to the plant and also bind it firmly to the soil. In logging areas, extra care must be taken to avoid erosion; forests are replanted soon after they are harvested.

F
Fire!

Forest fires destroy thousands of plants, animals and homes every year. These fires burn hot enough to melt a car and travel faster than any human or animal can run. Lightning starts some of these fires, but people start most of them. A spark from a car or an ember from a campfire can set an entire forest ablaze.

Forestry workers sometimes light fires to help the forest heal. These controlled fires destroy sick trees or clean up piles of slash— leftover treetops, branches and waste wood from logging. This helps prepare a site for planting.

G

Grinding over gravel, graders groom good roads.

In remote areas, roads have to be planned and built before logging can begin. Powerful machines clear the way by removing boulders and stumps, digging ditches, and raising the center of the road so it can drain. Dump trucks spread gravel, and graders maintain the road by grooming out—leveling—bumps and potholes.

H

Horses and helicopters harvest trees on high hills.

Teams of large strong horses can haul logs from the forest to a landing. Although horses do little damage to the forest environment (and even provide some natural fertilizer), horse logging is slower than logging with machinery.

Helicopters can remove logs from very steep places, but they are expensive to buy and to fly.

I

Insects infest forests in cycles.

Millions of insects live in a healthy forest. Some are helpful; others are harmful, but all insects provide food for birds and other animals. Sometimes a change in climate can cause certain insect populations, such as mountain pine beetles, to grow too large. These beetles usually attack only older or damaged trees, but when they multiply too quickly, they can turn a green forest to rusty red.

J

Jammed logs must be jostled loose.

Moving logs on water can be quicker than hauling them by road or railway. Logs float easily, but they can also get jammed together. In the past, it was common to see rivers full of logs floating to a mill. Skilled workers wearing waterproof caulk boots used long sharp poles to free any jammed logs and send them on their way. Today there are no more river drives, though many logs still travel on lakes and oceans.

K

King-sized kilns dry many kinds of lumber.

Logs are cut into boards while they are fresh and sappy. These boards have to dry out before they can be used, or they will twist and curl. Anything built with "green" lumber can pull apart as the wood dries.

An inch-thick board can take a year to dry, so freshly sawn lumber is stacked in large, very hot buildings known as kilns. Kiln-dried boards can be ready to ship to market in only a few days.

L

Loaded logging trucks leave the landing.

At the landing, machines load logs onto trucks that haul them away to become boards, plywood or paper. In the mill yard, the logs are weighed and measured and then stacked—decked—into piles. Heavy logs must be stacked so the piles don't shift or collapse. Decking logs can be as tricky as lifting giant pick-up sticks.

M

Millwrights work midnight to morning.

Lumber, plywood and pulp and paper mills often run both day and night. Special mechanics called millwrights keep them running safely. Sometimes a mill is shut down completely late at night so millwrights can repair the machinery. The hours after midnight when the screeching saws are silent can be a millwright's busiest time.

N

Nursery trees nestle near natural seedlings.

In a harvested area, some young trees—seedlings—grow back naturally, but others have to be planted. Helicopter crews gather seed cones from the tops of evergreen trees like pine, spruce and fir. Cone-pickers strip the sticky cones from the bits of broken branches. Seeds from these cones are planted in greenhouses or nurseries. After at least a year, the seedlings are lifted from their growing trays and frozen for the winter. This helps them get ready to live outdoors.

O

Old growth offers homes for owls, ospreys and others.

In mild climates, some old-growth trees are enormous. In drier climates, trees are much smaller, even if they are hundreds of years old. Some plants and animals are best suited to live in the shade of old forests. Others, like deer and moose, prefer to make their homes in younger, sunnier forests.

P

Perfect peelers are picked to make plywood.

While smaller trees can be pulped to make paper, plywood is made from large straight trees. These trees—peelers—are soaked or steamed to make them easier to work with. A long knife blade unwinds each log into thin sheets, like peeling giant-sized paper towels from a roll. The cut sheets are dried, layered, glued and pressed so they will stay flat. Plywood can be used for building almost anything from sailboats to schools.

Q

Quiet settles quickly after quitting time.

In the early days of logging, and for many modern forest workers, quitting time means heading back to camp. In camp, crews clean up, eat, get their tools ready for the next day and, perhaps, wash their sweaty socks.

Work begins at first light, so bedtime comes early. The camp grows quiet, except for the whispers of the wind, the distant howls of coyotes—and the snoring.

R

Replanting renews a rich resource.

Unlike oil or gas that can be used up, trees are a renewable resource. A forest can reseed itself or be replanted. Experienced tree planters can plant over a thousand trees a day. Each seedling has a "plug" of earth and fertilizer around its roots to help it get a good start. When carefully planted, these seedlings will grow straight and tall.

S

Silviculture is the science of forestry.

Silviculture is the art and science of caring for forests to make sure they stay healthy and continue to grow. At universities and in the forest itself, students learn the natural habits and needs of each type of tree, as well as how trees live together with other plants and animals. Silviculture students also learn the best ways to manage a forest so it can be harvested again and again.

T

Timber cruisers tally trees.

Foresters study each area—known as a block—before it is logged. Is the land flat or hilly? What kinds of trees grow there? How many? It would be impossible to check every tree, so forest workers called timber cruisers study sample areas. They count—tally—all the trees and record their type, height, age, diameter and condition.

U

Undergrowth covers the ground under the forest canopy.

The forest forms a green umbrella—a canopy—which protects everything under it. In turn, the undergrowth helps the trees by keeping the earth moist. Bacteria and fungi in the undergrowth also help fallen trees, leaves and other organic matter to decay and become fertilizer for new growth.

V

Value-added work creates vital jobs.

Value-added means adding value to a natural resource. All natural resources—like forests, oceans and oil fields—create jobs. Loggers and mill workers depend on the forest for jobs, but so do carpenters, cabinetmakers and craftsmen. Trees can be made into hundreds of value-added products, from paper to guitars to sundecks to log homes.

W

Weekends can be workdays on a woodlot.

A woodlot is a piece of forested public land. Caretakers of this land harvest and replant it, much as a farmer does his fields. Although there is always work to be done on a woodlot, it can still be a good place to picnic, camp under the stars, collect firewood or simply enjoy the forest "for rest."

X

2 x 4s, 2 x 6s and 2 x 8s are stacked in the back of a 4 x 4.

A rough-cut board, a 2 x 4 (2 by 4), is two inches thick and four inches wide. Rough-cut means the board has been sawn but not yet smoothed. A finished 2 x 4 is actually 1.5 x 3.5 inches!

These boards may arrive at building sites in the back of powerful four-wheel-drive trucks (4 by 4s or 4 x 4s).

Y

Yellow and red cedar yield to the yarder.

Both yellow and red cedar grow well in wet climates. Their wood is light, flexible and slow to rot. For centuries, First Nations people made masks, dishes, hunting bows, arrows, totem poles, homes and canoes from this sweet-smelling wood.

To harvest cedar in steep mountain areas, loggers use a tall crane-like machine—a yarder—to move the logs to the landing because ordinary skidders could tip over.

Z

Zooming dozer boats zip through a maze of logs.

When logs are moved on large lakes or oceans, they are sorted and chained together into big rafts—booms—for tugboats to pull away. Boom men once leapt from log to log, poking and prodding the logs into place. Modern crews also use boom or dozer boats to do this work. These small but powerful boats push, shove and herd logs so they can be gathered into booms or loaded onto barges to begin a journey that could take them around the world.

Fast Forestry Facts

A Trees are among the oldest, tallest and largest living things on Earth. The world's tallest living tree is a redwood that measures nearly 400 feet or 120 meters.

B Breakup can last up to two months. These months may be the only time off loggers have all year.

C Crews must make sure they load everything they will need for the day into the crummy: tools, mosquito repellent, lunches, snacks, water bottles, rain gear and dry clothes.

D Many logging-truck drivers leave for work at three in the morning. They pick up their first load of logs in the bush and deliver it to the mill before most people have breakfast.

E After logging, crews plant fast-growing grass and clover on landings and logging roads to protect the freshly exposed soil.

F Helicopters, planes and satellites are used to spot forest fires, although sometimes people still watch for and report new fires from lookout towers.

G In cold climates, winter logging roads can be built on ice or packed snow. These roads disappear in the spring.

H Horses and helicopters never work together because helicopters frighten even the biggest horses.

I As bark beetles bore into a tree, the tree fights back, filling the beetles' tunnels with sap. These pockets of sap on the bark are the first signs of a beetle attack.

J The art of balancing on a floating log (log birling) is kept alive today through logger sports, where staying upright on a slippery floating log is a competitive event.

K The average temperature inside a lumber kiln is 220° Fahrenheit or 100° Celsius.

L Modern sawmills have lasers and computers that scan each log before cutting it to make maximum use of the wood.

M Mills usually have three eight-hour working shifts, two during the day and the "graveyard" shift from midnight to eight in the morning.

N Helicopter crews sometimes collect seed cones by lowering a large mesh basket with a rotating wire brush. The brush rakes the cones into the basket.

O In a natural forest, shrubs and fast-growing, broad-leafed trees are the first to grow. Slower-growing trees get their start in the shade of these original plants.

P Peeler logs can be hard to find, so sometimes strands (flakes) of wood are layered with wax and resin glue to make a wood product called OSB—oriented strand board—that can be used instead of plywood.

Q In the early days, when loggers used only horses or oxen to skid logs, these animals also stayed in bush camps with the crews.

R Tree planters wear planting bags with three pouches so they can carry bundles of seedlings as well as drinking water and rain gear.

S Silviculture students spend many days on "field trips" so they can learn directly from the forest as well as from textbooks.

T From timber cruisers' samples, foresters make up a plan that includes where and how to build roads, what kind of logging practices to use and what trees to plant.

U A forest is a complete ecosystem: everything in it, from mushrooms to treetops, depends on and helps everything else.

V Forests also add value to many, many lives as any hiker, camper, fisherman or birdwatcher knows.

W The caretaker of a woodlot follows strict rules for harvesting, cleaning up, replanting and thinning the forest.

X Japan uses the metric system in building, so the lumber shipped there is cut in millimeters, not inches.

Y Yellow cedar is also called cypress. It grows slowly and can take over two hundred years to mature.

Z A dozer boat is a small boom boat.

Acknowledgments

Authors' Note:
Forest practices vary greatly from region to region. We have focused on the type of forestry we see around us every day.

Many thanks to the following people who helped with research, offered advice, gave generously and enthusiastically of their time and kept us from getting lost in the forest:

Dirk Allen, BC coastal logger, heavy-equipment operator (crane); **Ann Baker**, silviculture technician; **Gabe, Karel** and **Rob Bergen**, tree planters; **bill bissett**, poet; **Gladys Bontron**, camp cook; **Ian Briggs**, Registered Professional Forester (RPF), president, Montane Forest Consultants Ltd.; **Clancys'** restaurant for giving us a place to meet; **Barbara J. Coupé**, RPF; **Ed Deleau**, Latourneau operator; **Ken Drushka**, writer and columnist, forestry issues; **Lorne Dufour**, poet, horse logger; **Geoff Ellen**, agrologist; **Dave Flear**, timber cruiser, forestry consultant, woodlot licensee; **Patrick Friesen**, poet; **Kelly Powell**, RPF, operations forester for West Fraser Mills Ltd., 100 Mile House; **Tom Redl**, woodlot manager, West Fraser Mills Ltd.; **Dale Richter**, RPF; **Bob Schmidt**, MSc (wood science); **Mike Simpson**, RPF, Montane Forest Consultants Ltd.; **John Stace-Smith**, RPF, Tolko Industries Ltd.; **Joel Steinberg**, independent logger, planting foreman; **Levi Waldron**, PhD (wood science and environmental studies); **Mark Waldron**, woodlot licensee; **John Walsh**, resident linguist, weekend logger; **George White**, silviculture superintendent; **Carol Wierstra**, cabinetmaker, co-founder of Cariboo-made Value Added Society; **Cindy Wickingstad**, millworker, chip car operator, third-generation lumber grader; **Dave Wickingstad**, millwright; **Olivia Wilkins**, PhD candidate (cell and systems biology), specializing in forestry; **Gernot Zemanek**, owner/operator of Roserim Forest Nursery, woodlot licensee; **Damon Zirnhelt**, MA (development economics), managing partner, Zirnhelt Timber Frames; **David Zirnhelt**, former BC Minister of Forests, land use consultant, woodlot licensee; **Sam Zirnhelt**, RPF, BSc (natural resource management), MSc (forestry), managing partner, Zirnhelt Timber Frames.

—Kathleen Cook Waldron and Ann Walsh

Thanks also to the following:

Arnt Arntzen and The Wood Co-op, BCIT Forest Resources Technician Program, Benwell Atkins, Bruno Tramph and L&M Lumber Co. Ltd., Chasm Contracting, Daniel Stickel—luthier, Earl Sanford Logging Ltd., Folklore Contracting Ltd., George and Janie LaBrash, Gernot Zemanek family, Gulf Log Salvage, Kelly Powell and West Fraser Timber Co. Ltd., Lorne Dufour, McNeil and Sons Logging Ltd., Mission Municipal Forest, PRT Pelton Reforestation Ltd., HomeWorx, Harken Towing Co. Ltd., Pacific Pallet Ltd., Terry Horne and Mary Durocher, Williams Lake Plywood (a division of West Fraser Mills Ltd.), Xa:ytem Interpretive Centre and the many men and women who shared their knowledge and expertise, and helped me record the images for this book.

—Bob Warick